# All New Superstar Kids

## Rhyming moral fun!

Written by Gavin Rhodes
Illustrated by Aliyah Coreana

Published by New Generation Publishing in 2017

Copyright © Gavin Rhodes 2017
Illustrated by Aliyah Coreana

First Edition

ISBN: 978-1-78719-630-8

www.newgeneration-publishing.com

New Generation Publishing

# Contents Page

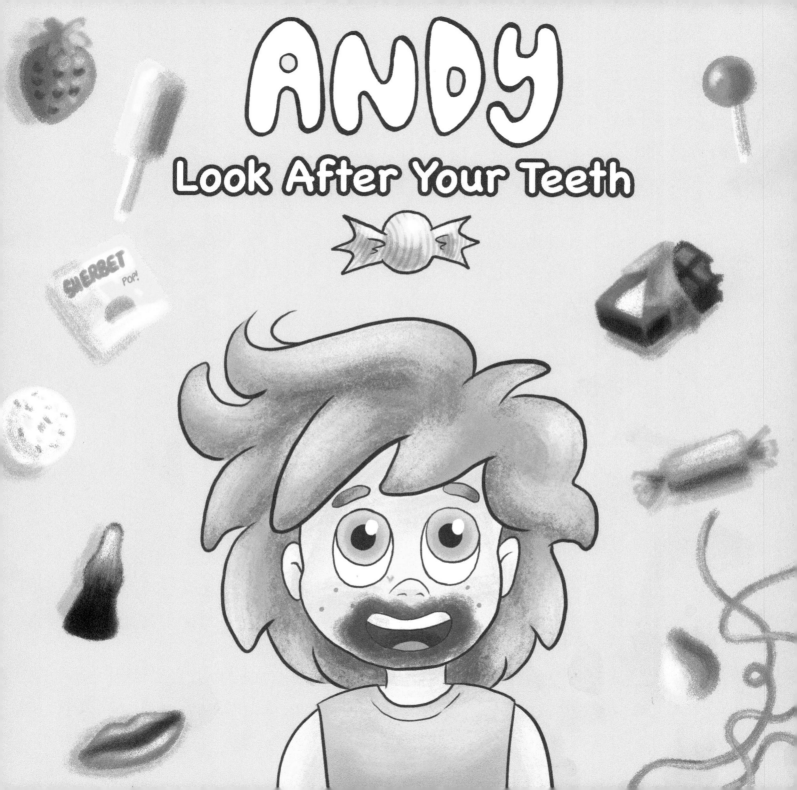

All kids love CANDY,
But no kid loves candy more than ANDY.

Andy would eat all kinds of candy, from...
Cherry LIPS
  to Sherbet DIPS,
    Fruity JELLIES
      to Chocolate PENNIES,
        PEARDROPS

to LOLLIPOPS,
  Strawberry SOURS,
  to giant gobstoppers that last for HOURS.

Andy certainly had a sweet TOOTH,
  He once ate candy for
  breakfast and that's the TRUTH!

Andy's parents would often SHOUT...
'Stop eating sweets, your teeth will fall OUT!'

One day, whilst chewing on a fizzy cola BAR,
Andy suddenly let out an almighty ARRRGH!!!!

ARGH!

The pain in Andy's tooth was
almost too much to TAKE.
With all those sweets, it's no
surprise he got TOOTHACHE.

Andy's mum said he had to go to the dentist...
Andy wasn't keen but he showed WILLING.
The dentist wasn't scary but he said, 'You need a FILLING.'

The filling didn't hurt in the SLIGHTEST,
And now Andy's teeth were pain free and at their WHITEST.
Andy didn't want any more tooth PAIN,
Nor did he fancy having fillings at the dentist AGAIN.

It was time to cut down on all those SWEETS,
So Andy started to eat healthier TREATS.

Rather than liquorice and
candy of green, blue and RED,
He ate bananas, apples and
grapes INSTEAD.

Eating sugary treats is OKAY,

But not too many, and you

must remember to brush

your teeth twice a DAY.

Harry never wanted to go to BED,
He just wanted to stay up and play with his toys INSTEAD.

Harry's parents struggled to get him to bed every NIGHT,
And by the time he gave in, it was almost LIGHT!

Bedtime was always the same...
'Harry go to bed NOW!'
'I'm playing with Superstar Man.
Bosh, bang, POW!!!'

Harry would always DELAY,
'We know your game!' his parents would SAY.

Harry's mum was puzzled... 'Do you think Harry has an allergy to his BED?!'
'Maybe that's why his eyes are always RED!'

'No dear!' replied Harry's dad...
'By going to bed early he
thinks he's missing OUT.'
'It's all very silly but
that's what it's ABOUT.'

Harry's dad sat down
next to Harry...
'You need to go to bed
when you are told SON,
Feeling tired all day
really is no FUN.'

YAWN!

'But I'm not tired,' said Harry
with a great big YAWN.
'Oh yes you are!' replied Harry's dad,
'That's what happens when you
go to bed at DAWN!'

The next day in school, Harry was SNORING!
'I'm sorry Harry,' yelled his teacher, 'Is this BORING?!'

All the children laughed out LOUD,
Harry blushed, he was not PROUD!

Harry no longer wanted to feel TIRED,
He realised that maybe more sleep was REQUIRED.

From that day on, Harry went

to bed when he was TOLD,

Although Superstar Man,

he had to HOLD!


So... don't feel frazzled,

grumpy and LAZY,

Get lots of sleep and you'll

be fresh as a DAISY.

# Nikki

## *Patience*

Nikki's personality was really GREAT,
But she had no patience, she just wouldn't WAIT.

Nikki had to be first in every QUEUE,
Waiting in line she did not like to DO.

Nikki's lack of patience meant when she read a BOOK,
She'd jump to the last few pages to take a sneaky LOOK.

Nikki was really CLEVER,
But everything in her life just seemed to take FOREVER!

'I want my jelly, has it SET?'
'Are we nearly there YET?'

'What's wrong with these flowers?! They're taking too long to GROW.'

'I need a new pet tortoise; this one's far too SLOW.'

'Mummy, when is dinner READY?'
'Why isn't he walking yet? Come on FREDDY!'

24

'I want it to be Christmas NOWWW!'
'But it's only October!' Nikki's mum said with a raised BROW.

One day Nikki was badgering her mum for TREATS.
'After dinner!' said Mum... 'I've made a lovely salad with a selection of MEATS.'

Nikki continued to PERSIST,

She simply didn't get the GIST.


Mum got cross and as

she put down her PLATE,

She said, 'Honestly Nikki,

you must learn to WAIT!'

Nikki ignored her mum's ADVICE,
Now there was no dinner, no treats or anything NICE.

Banished from the kitchen, Nikki sat in her room and had a sulk and a GRUMBLE.
Then suddenly from her stomach came a great big RUMBLE!

Nikki didn't want to go to bed without dinner in her TUMMY,
She realised that having no patience was silly and apologised to MUMMY.

Nikki was a lot more patient from then on it's fair to SAY,
She didn't even look for presents before Christmas DAY.

Nikki's new found patience was certainly WORTHWHILE...
Rewarded with a beautiful cake; now that made her SMILE!

Patience is a virtue as the saying GOES,
And good things come to those who wait... as this story clearly SHOWS.

# SASKIA

## TAKING CARE

Saskia was a very active and carefree CHILD,
Just like a monkey in the WILD.

Wherever Saskia went she
would run, climb and JUMP,
But there was often a trip,
fall or a BUMP.

Every day she would end up
scratched or BRUISED,
Leaving her parents
far from AMUSED.

Saskia had no worries or FEARS,
Warnings of caution or
safety would fall on deaf EARS.

Saskia was always being told to be more sensible and AWARE,
But she never listened, she just didn't CARE.

One morning Saskia was playing with her
ball when, into a busy road it BOUNCED,
And without hesitation Saskia POUNCED.

A car was approaching mightily FAST,
Saskia stopped suddenly and the car went zooming PAST.

'Gosh,' gasped Saskia...'That was SCARY!'
It was then that Saskia realised she must be more WARY.

Saskia's parents were cross but glad she was ALRIGHT,
They gave her a list of safety tips to read that NIGHT...

Never run into a road or on a TRACK,
Never drink from a glass with a CRACK.
Never throw SAND,
Never run with a pointy object in your HAND.
Never play with forks and KNIVES,
Never go too close to BEEHIVES.
Never climb a wobbly LEDGE,
Never play near the water's EDGE.
Always wear a seat belt in the CAR,
When playing in the park— never go FAR.
Never go near fire or other hot DANGERS,
And never, ever, ever talk to STRANGERS.

No matter your age or SIZE,
It's important to be sensible and
a little STREETWISE.

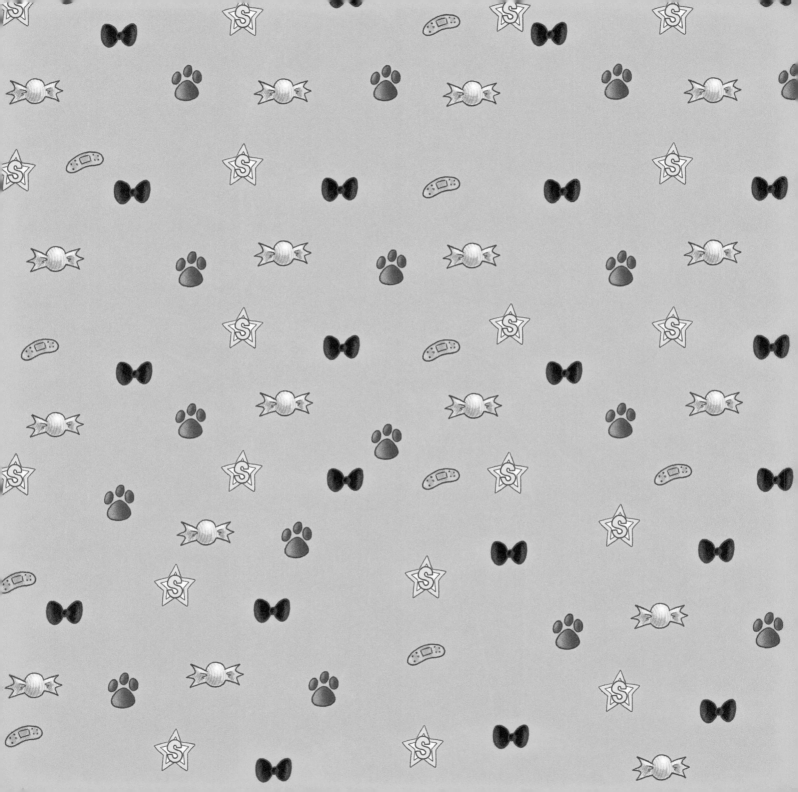

Ravi longed for a dog as a PET,
His parents would say, 'Maybe when
you're older but not just YET.'

Ravi watched others taking their dogs
for walks on their LEADS,
All different shapes, sizes and BREEDS.

Dogs were here, dogs were THERE.
Dogs, it seemed, were EVERYWHERE.

Beagle

Daschund

German Shepherd

Dalmation

Labrador

Poodle

Ravi just didn't understand why he wasn't allowed a four legged FRIEND,
He was driving his parents round the BEND.

'Mum, why can't I have a dog yet? I'm 6 and a HALF.'
'Because you can't even look after yourself,'
said Mum, 'Now, get in the BATH!'

The next morning the phone rang EARLY,
It was dear Great Aunt SHIRLEY.

'Hello Rita, I'm off on holiday
for a week, can you look
after my dog, DAPPY?'

'Okay,' said Ravi's mum, 'I know
someone who'll be very HAPPY!'

The next day Dappy arrived and Ravi was so excited for him to STAY,

He couldn't wait to take him outside and PLAY.

Every day Ravi and Dappy would play fetch with a BONE,

And Ravi knew for sure now that he wanted a dog of his OWN.

Every evening however,
Dappy was scratching and
barking at the DOOR,
'Mum can you take him out,'
said Ravi, 'My feet are SORE.'

Ravi's mum was less
than IMPRESSED,
'Let's take him out together
and *then* you can REST.'

Ravi hadn't fully understood
what having a dog would MEAN,
It was a lot more involved
than he had FORESEEN.

Walkies, feeding and
sweeping dog HAIR,
Dappy needed a lot of
attention, love and CARE.

As the week went on, Ravi cared
for Dappy like he was his OWN,
He did everything for Dappy
and he didn't even MOAN.

Ravi's mum was so pleased
he'd been a responsible BOY,
And she could see that a dog
would bring them both lots of JOY.

So remember... a pet is more than just a little
buddy you can play with as you WISH,
Pets need lots of looking after whether
it's a dog, a cat or a FISH.

Gavin, a family man with a passion for sports and the arts, started writing the 'Superstar Kids' series in 2015 on his commute to and from the city. Fun, rhyming stories with important life messages for children formed the basis of Superstar Kids, with inspiration coming from his children and experiences of parenthood.

Aliyah is a creative artist with a passion for drawing and portraying all things colourful! Her inspiration comes from video games and animation. She strives to depict diversity through her work because she understands the importance of representation, especially for children in the present day.

For more information on Superstar Kids please visit....
Website: www.superstarkidsbook.com
Instagram: www.instagram/superstar_kids_books
Facebook: www.facebook.com/superstarkidsbook

We would love to hear your feedback with a review online or drop us an email at superstarkids.book@gmail.com

The original 'Superstar Kids' Rhyming Moral Fun is also available to order online through Amazon and all other good book retailers.

Lightning Source UK Ltd.
Milton Keynes UK
UKHW02f2031280118
316892UK00006B/85/P